SOFIA MARTINEZ

The Missing Mouse

by Jacqueline Jules

illustrated by Kim Smith

PICTURE WINDOW BOOKS
a capstone imprint

Sofia Martinez is published by
Picture Window Books, a Capstone Imprint
1710 Roe Crest Drive
North Mankato, MN 56003
www.capstonepub.com

Library of Congress Cataloging-in-Publication Data
Jules, Jacqueline, 1956- author.
The missing mouse / by Jacqueline Jules ; illustrated
by Kim Smith.
pages cm. -- (Sofia Martinez)

Summary: Sofia is temporarily entrusted with
Snowflake the class mouse — but he escapes, and she
and her sisters must figure out a way to catch him.

ISBN 978-1-4795-5774-5 (library binding)
ISBN 978-1-4795-5778-3 (pbk.)
ISBN 978-1-4795-6206-0 (ebook)

1. Mice — Juvenile fiction. 2. Sisters — Juvenile
fiction. 3. Hispanic Americans — Juvenile fiction.
[1. Mice —Fiction. 2. Sisters —Fiction. 3. Hispanic
Americans —Fiction.] I. Smith, Kim, 1986- illustrator.
II. Title.
PZ7.J92947Mi 2015   [E]—dc23
                                     2014024411

Designer: Kay Fraser

Printed and bound in the United States of America.
052017   010540R

TABLE OF CONTENTS

Chapter 1
Meet Snowflake 5

Chapter 2
The Lost Mouse 14

Chapter 3
The Mouse Trap 20

CHAPTER 1

Meet Snowflake

Sofia heard a knock at the door and rushed to answer it. It was Albert. He came every Friday afternoon to take piano lessons with Sofia's mom.

Today Albert had a shoe box with him. And Sofia knew exactly what was in that shoe box.

"Hola, Sofia," Albert said.

"¡Hola! Is that Snowflake?"
Sofia asked.

"¡Sí!" Albert said proudly. "I'm
the very first person to take care of
our class pet."

"You are so lucky," Sofia said.

"But we have a problem."

"What?" Albert asked.

"Fur makes Mamá sneeze,"
Sofia said.

"Really?" Albert asked.

"Sí," Sofia said. "Our cat had to move to a new house."

"What should I do?" Albert asked. "My piano lesson starts in a few minutes!"

"Don't worry," Sofia said. "I'll take care of Snowflake."

"Are you sure?" Albert asked, looking worried.

"No hay problema," Sofia said, smiling.

Albert wasn't so sure, but he didn't have any other options.

"Snowflake likes to escape. Please don't let him run away," Albert said.

"Got it," Sofia said.

Sofia took the box downstairs. Luisa and Elena, Sofia's older sisters, were watching TV.

"¿Qué tienes?" Luisa asked.

"A mouse," Sofia said. "His name is Snowflake."

"Whose is it?" Luisa asked.

"It is Albert's class pet," Sofia said. Luisa looked impressed. Elena looked bored.

"I think Snowflake wants to see what we are watching," Sofia said.

She slowly lifted the lid. The white mouse stood up on his back legs. He squeaked.

"How cute!" Sofia laughed.

"He is cute!" Luisa agreed.

"Please be quiet," Elena said. "I'm trying to watch my show."

"Okay, okay," Sofia said.

Sofia was just about to close the lid when Snowflake jumped out of the box.

"NO!" Sofia screamed.

CHAPTER 2

The Lost Mouse

Snowflake ran across the floor and under the big chair.

"Aaahhh!" her sisters screamed.

"¡Ayúdame!" Sofia cried.

"No way!" Elena shouted. "I'm telling Mamá!"

"You can't!" Luisa said.

The Martinez sisters knew better than to bother Mamá when she was teaching piano lessons.

"We should call Abuela," Sofia decided. "She always knows how to fix things."

"Well, you better do something fast," Elena said. "We don't have much time."

Sofia ran across the room to get the phone.

Sofia listened carefully for several minutes. Then she thanked her abuela and hung up.

"Good news! All we need is a bucket," Sofia said.

"¿Para qué?" Elena asked.

"To catch Snowflake," Sofia said. "It should be pretty easy."

"Mamá has one in the laundry room," Luisa said. "I'll get it."

When Luisa came back, the girls stared at the bucket.

"Abuela says to put food for the mouse inside," Sofia said.

"Okay. What do mice eat?" Luisa asked.

"Cheese," Elena said.

"That is a problem," Luisa said, pointing at the ceiling. "The cheese is upstairs in the kitchen."

The sounds of Albert on the piano came through. There was no way they could get to the kitchen without being noticed.

"That is not going to work," Elena said.

"No te preocupes. I'll go across the yard to Tía Carmen's," Sofia said. "¡Adiós!"

CHAPTER 3

The Mouse Trap

A few minutes later, Sofia was back with her cousin Hector.

"I'm back, and I brought help," she said proudly.

"I really just want to see the mouse," Hector said.

"First we have to catch him," Elena said. "Did you bring some cheese?"

"No," Hector said. "We are out of cheese."

"We brought peanut butter instead," Sofia said.

"Peanut butter?" Elena said.

"Mamá said mice like it just as much as cheese," Hector added.

Sofia smeared peanut butter inside the bucket. Then she put the bucket near the big chair.

"The bucket is too tall for a mouse," Hector said. "How will he get in?"

"We need stairs," Sofia said. "Grab my blocks, Hector."

Sofia and Hector started building the stairs. They worked fast.

Soon the bucket trap was ready.

Sofia, Luisa, Elena, and Hector

hid near the chair and watched.

No one made a sound. They saw

Snowflake run out.

Snowflake stood on his back legs and sniffed. He began to climb. Then they heard the mouse plop in the bucket.

"¡Lo hicimos!" Sofia shouted.

Just then, Albert opened the door. "Where's Snowflake?"

"¡Aquí!" Sofia proudly pointed at the bucket.

Albert scooped up the mouse. "You said you wouldn't let him run away."

"¡Yo sé! He didn't run away," Sofia said. "He had an adventure."

"So did we," Elena said.

Snowflake squeaked, and everybody laughed — even Albert.

Spanish Glossary

abuela — grandma

adiós — goodbye

aquí — here

ayúdame — help me

hola — hello

lo hicimos — we did it

mamá — mom

no hay problema — no problem

no te preocupes — don't worry

para qué — for what

qué tienes — what do you have

sí — yes

tía — aunt

yo sé — I know

Talk It Out

1. Do you think it's a good idea to have a class pet? Why or why not?

2. How did you think Sofia would catch Snowflake? Were you surprised by her plan? Why or why not?

3. Do you think Sofia told her mom about the mouse and what happened? Explain your answer and reasoning.

Write It Down

1. Sofia loses Snowflake when he jumps out of the box. Write about a time when you lost something.

2. Pretend you are Snowflake. Using his point of view, write a story about his adventure at Sofia's house.

3. Pick your three favorite Spanish words or phrases from the story. Write three sentences using what you learned.

About the Author

Jacqueline Jules is the award-winning author of twenty-five children's books, including *No English* (2012 Forward National Literature Award), *Zapato Power: Freddie Ramos Takes Off* (2010 CYBILS Literary Award, Maryland Blue Crab Young Reader Honor Award, and ALSC Great Early Elementary Reads), and *Freddie Ramos Makes a Splash* (named on 2013 List of Best Children's Books of the Year by Bank Street College Committee).

When not reading, writing, or teaching, Jacqueline enjoys time with her family in Northern Virginia.

About the Illustrator

Kim Smith has worked in magazines, advertising, animation, and children's gaming. She studied illustration at the Alberta College of Art and Design in Calgary, Alberta.

Kim is the illustrator of the upcoming middle-grade mystery series *The Ghost and Max Monroe*, the picture book *Over the River and Through the Woods*, and the cover of the forthcoming middle-grade novel *How to Make a Million*. She resides in Calgary, Alberta.

FUN
doesn't stop here!

- Videos & Contests
- Games & Puzzles
- Friends & Favorites
- Authors & Illustrators

Discover more at
www.capstonekids.com

See you soon!

¡Nos Vemos pronto!